Pizza for Sam

Written by **Mary Labatt**

Illustrated by **Marisol Sarrazin**

SCHOLASTIC INC.
New York Toronto London Auckland Sydney
Mexico City New Delhi Hong Kong Buenos Aires

✪ Kids Can Read ™

Kids Can Read is a trademark of Kids Can Press

ISBN 0-439-58743-3

12 11 10 9 8 7 6 5 4 3 2 1   3 4 5 6 7 8/0

Printed in the U.S.A.   23

First Scholastic printing, September 2003

Edited by David MacDonald

Designed By Stacie Bowes and Marie Bartholomew

Joan and Bob were having a party.

They made food.

No one made food for Sam.

The doorbell rang.

Joan and Bob ran to the door.

Sam ran, too.

Sam saw cake and cookies

and pie and chips.

"This is good," thought Sam.

"I need food."

Joan and Bob put the food

on the table.

Sam sniffed.

"YUM!" thought Sam.

"This is good food."

Sam jumped on a chair.

She sniffed the cake.

"I like cake," thought Sam.

"Cake is good for puppies."

But Bob saw her.

"NO, Sam!" he cried.

"Cake is not for puppies!"

"Woof!" said Sam.

She flopped on the floor.

"I need food.

I need food for puppies."

Sam jumped back

on the chair.

She sniffed the cookies.

"I like cookies," thought Sam.

"Cookies are good for puppies."

But Joan saw her.

"NO, Sam!" she cried.

"Cookies are not for puppies."

"Woof!" said Sam.

She flopped on the floor.

"I need food.

I need food for puppies."

Sam jumped back

on the chair.

She sniffed the pie.

"I like pie," thought Sam.

"Pie is good for puppies."

But Joan and Bob saw her.

"NO, Sam!" they cried.

"Pie is not for puppies!"

"Woof!" said Sam.

She flopped on the floor.

"I need food.

I need food for puppies!"

Sam went to her bowl.

She put her chin on her paws.

She closed her eyes

and started to dream.

Sam dreamed of cake

and cookies

and pie and chips.

Lots of chips!

Bob came back.

Sam opened her eyes.

"Are you hungry, Sam?" he asked.

Sam jumped up.

"You bet!" she thought.

"Bring on the food."

Bob went to the kitchen.

He came back

with Sam's bowl.

Sam sniffed.

"YUCK!" thought Sam.

"This is dog food!"

"Dog food stinks!

I hate dog food!"

Sam was sad.

"Dog food is NOT for puppies!"

The doorbell rang.

Joan and Bob ran to the door.

Sam ran, too.

A man had a big box.

"Pizza!" said the man.

Sam sniffed and sniffed.

"What is pizza?" thought Sam.

"It does not smell

like cake or cookies.

It does not smell

like pie or chips.

Best of all,

it does NOT smell like dog food!"

Joan put the box on the table.

The doorbell rang.

The telephone rang, too.

Joan went one way.

Bob went the other way.

Sam looked at the box.

She looked around.

Everyone was busy.

Sam dragged the box

behind the sofa.

She scratched the box

and chewed the box.

"Gr-r-r-r."

At last, the box was open!

Sam took a big bite.

"YUM!" she thought.

"This is good food!"

"Cake is not for puppies.

Cookies are not for puppies.

Pie is not for puppies.

Dog food is not for puppies.

I know what is for puppies ..."

"Pizza is for puppies!"